The Crab Man

Patricia E. Van West

illustrations by Cedric Lucas

Turtle Books

NEW YORK

"Gotcha," Neville said as he reached into the bush and snatched up a small brown object. It tickled his hand as it tried to escape, but Neville held on. Gently, he lowered it into the shoe box with the other three hermit crabs. Two more to go.

The boy spent the next half hour searching the bushes until the last two crabs were captured. Then using an old piece of screen as a lid, he headed off to meet the crab man.

From a distance Neville could see the crab man standing in front of the hotel gate talking to the guard. Inside the gates, a group of tourists was boarding a bus.

Perhaps these tourists would climb Dunn's River Falls or go rafting down the Martha Brae River. They might even tour the sugar cane plantation where Neville's father worked. The island of Jamaica depended on tourists. And now Neville depended on them, too.

"Six?" the crab man asked as Neville approached.

Neville nodded as he handed over the box.

The crab man lifted the screen and started poking and jabbing each crab. When he was satisfied, he picked up an old black gym bag and dumped the crabs inside. Then he reached into his pocket and handed a crumpled U.S. dollar to Neville.

Every day for a week, Neville had brought the crab man six crabs. And every day, Neville had taken home a U.S. dollar. Even though Neville's father worked in the sugar cane fields, there was little money for extras. Neville was saving his crab money to buy a new dress for his mother—a fancy one the color of the sea.

Still, Neville worried about his crabs. They were his friends. He loved to sit as still as a rock and watch them scamper in the dirt. Sometimes they would crawl over his bare feet and tickle so much that his loud laughter sent them darting into their shells.

The following day, after Neville handed over six more crabs, the crab man said, "My helper's sick. Do his work and I'll pay you an extra dollar." Then the crab man hurried toward the gates of the hotel.

Not only did Neville want the dollar, but he was curious to go through the hotel gates. As he hurried after the crab man, the guard reached out to stop Neville. But one nod from the crab man and suddenly Neville had entered the hotel grounds.

Crossing a grove of coconut trees, Neville saw a gigantic swimming pool surrounded by lounge chairs and tourists. It was there the crab man stopped, lowering his gym bag beside a large, white circle painted on the concrete deck.

"Place your bets, place your bets. It's time for c-r-r-r-r-ab r-r-r-r-acing," announced the crab man in a loud voice.

Tourists wandered toward the circle.

GRANVILLE COUNTY LIBRARY SYSTEM
P.O. BOX 339
OXFORD, NC 27565

"Here," said the crab man thrusting a small dirty box into Neville's hands. "Dump these crabs in the center of the circle when I say 'go.'"

Reaching the middle of the circle, Neville lifted the lid of the airless box and peered inside. There were six crabs, tucked tightly in their shells. Not dull, brown shells, but brightly painted shells: blue, red, yellow, green, silver, and orange.

"Pick your color! Pick your color!" shouted the crab man. Tourists lined up to place their bets. Then they gathered around the circle, waiting for the race to begin.

The crab man gave Neville the signal. Neville shook the crabs onto the hot concrete as gently as he could and backed away. People cheered as the red crab began to crawl toward the circle's edge. Soon the other crabs began to move and more cheers were heard.

"Go blue!" shouted one woman.

"Come on, red!" yelled two young boys.

"Hi ho, silver," said a man as the silver crab neared the finish line.

More crab racing? Not with these crabs, Neville thought. He walked over to the crab man and said, "These crabs need water and a cool spot to rest."

"Chuh mon," said the crab man with a wave of his hand. "They're good for at least four more races."

Four more races! Neville's hands turned icy cold under the June sun.

Clutching the box of crabs to his chest, Neville started to run.

"Stop, mon!"

But it was too late. Neville dashed around the pool, past the staring tourists, through the grove of coconut trees, and out the gates of the hotel before the guard could stop him. On and on he ran, until he was safely home.

Neville rushed into the house. Throwing his
arms around his mother, he told her the story.
Wiping his tears, she asked, "What will you do?"

"If I stop selling crabs, I won't be able to
buy you a new dress," said Neville.

"I like crabs more than new dresses," his
mother said with a gentle smile.

Neville thought a moment. Then he hugged his mother before heading outside with the box of crabs. In the cool shade of the bushes, he opened the lid. One at a time, out they came, slowly but surely.

"Its time for c-r-r-r-r-ab r-r-r-r-acing," he whispered as the brightly painted crabs crawled across the dirt and into the bushes.

Author's Notes

Jamaica

The setting of *The Crab Man* is Jamaica. Jamaica, the third
largest island in the Caribbean Sea, is slightly smaller than the state of
Connecticut. Its climate is hot and tropical. This island is a popular
tourist spot because of its rugged mountains, tropical forests, magnificent
waterfalls, and miles of white sand beaches. In addition to tourism, many
Jamaicans are employed in agriculture (sugar, spices, and fruit) and
mining (bauxite and alumina). Although the Jamaican people come from
a variety of cultures, they all share the Jamaican motto: "Out of Many,
One People."

Hermit Crabs

Hermit crabs begin their lives as larva, swimming in the ocean.
After they grow legs, eyes, and body parts, they walk around the ocean
floor looking for empty shells to use as houses. After finding the perfect
home, they journey to shore. It only takes a few weeks on dry land for
hermit crabs to forget how to swim and metamorphose (change) into
air-breathing animals.

While they may be small, hermit crabs benefit the environment in
a big way. Using other creatures' empty shells makes them the perfect
recyclers. In addition, hermit crabs clean up the shoreline by eating
creatures that have died. Humans are the crabs' most dangerous enemy
because they can pollute the crabs' environment, destroy their habitat,
and collect them to sell in pet stores.

For my daughter, Kate— PV

To Diane, Jorrell, Jaleesa; to all who inspire— CL

Turtle
B O O K S

The Crab Man
Text copyright © 1998 by Patricia E. Van West
Illustrations copyright © 1998 by Cedric Lucas

Published in 1998 by Turtle Books

Turtle Books, 866 United Nations Plaza, Suite 525
New York, New York 10017

Cover and book design by Jessica Kirchoff Bowlby
Text of this book is set in Goudy Sans Medium
Illustrations are composed of pastel and casein on marble dust paper

First Edition
Printed on 80# White Mountie matte, acid-free paper
Smyth sewn, cambric reinforced binding
Printed and bound in the United States of America

10   9   8   7   6   5   4   3   2   1

Library of Congress Cataloging-in-Publication Data
Van West, Patricia E., 1952-
The Crab Man / Patricia E. Van West ; illustrated by Cedric Lucas.   p.   cm.
Summary: When Neville sees the hermit crabs which he so gently collected
being mistreated by the crab man at a Jamaican hotel, he no longer
wants to supply them but would thereby forfeit his income.
ISBN 1-890515-08-6 (hardcover : alk. paper)
[1. Hermit crabs—Fiction. 2. Crabs—Fiction. 3. Animals—Treatment—Fiction. 4. Jamaica—Fiction.]
I. Lucas, Cedric, ill.   II. Title. PZ7.V383Cr 1998 [E]—dc21 98-9679 CIP AC

Distributed by Publishers Group West

ISBN 1-890515-08-6